To Jack & Quinn

Thanks for supporting!

Love,
Bill William

The Adventures of Bree the Bee
The Radio Station

To Dee Moon Publishing
Young Minds Division

Atlanta, Georgia

Text Copyright © 2020 Bree Williams

Illustrations: Christina Rudenko

Manufactured in the United States of America.

ISBN: 978-1-7347224-3-7

Thank you to everyone who has made this possible:
Danielle LaVon and To Dee Moon Publishing,
My Co-Author Paola,
and my Illustrator Christina.

This book is dedicated to my brother, Todd Williams, who always encouraged me to strive for greatness.

THIS IS BREE THE BUMBLE BEE.
SHE LIVES IN A CHERRY TREE
with all of her family.

ONE DAY BREE LANDED
ON A PRETTY SUNFLOWER
AND NOTICED A WINDOW to a building was OPEN.
BREE BECAME CURIOUS
SO SHE FLEW INSIDE THE WINDOW.

Bree flew into the window
to find herself in a Radio Station.

Bree met Bill the Worker Bee
who worked at the Radio Station.
He showed her around the radio station.

First, He showed her A MICROPHONE
OR MICRÓFONO
A microphone is used for sound.
It makes the voices loud and clear so
that listeners can hear the music or
the workers voices.

NEXT, Bill turned on
the RECORDER OR GRABADORA
A recorder allows you to keep the sound
on a computer so that you can play it later.

THEN Bill showed her HEADPHONES OR AUDÍFONOS

Headphones are placed over your ears and used to hear sound that is playing. When you wear your headphones only you can hear the sounds.

There were large **SPEAKERS OR ALTAVOZ** in the radio station. Speakers are used for listening to sound so everyone can hear. You can play it loud or softly.

Bill the worker Bee had a **COMPUTER OR COMPUTADORA** on his desk. A computer is used to listen to music, watch videos and share pictures.

When the show started
Bill turned on the ON AIR LIGHT
OR LUZ AL AIRE.
An On Air light comes on to let
everyone know it is time
to be quiet so the radio show can begin.
Shhhhhh!

BREE THE BUMBLE BEE LEARNED SO MUCH while **VISTING THE RADIO STATION** She cannot wait to go back to the cherry tree and tell her family **WHAT SHE LEARNED.**

What did you learn while flying through the Radio Station with Bree the Bumblebee?

About the Author

Brianna "Bree" Williams was born and raised in Evansville, Indiana. She has an associate degree in Early Childhoon Education and a Bachelor's in Communication Studies. Upon graduating she wanted to find a way to put her two degrees together, and a children's book was birthed.

Bree is very excited to share her love of children and her career all in one. She hopes you and your family enjoy the adventures of Bree the Bee.

Made in the USA
Coppell, TX
25 February 2021